Welcome to tl
Juniper and E
at The Blooming Barn!

Sweet Peas and Bees
1st Edition, published May 2023
Copyright © 2023 Illustrated by Fiona Van Housen. Written and read by Mary Murphy. All rights reserved.
www.thebloomingbarn.com
www.marymurphy.ca

Published by Dove Creek Studios

While the Juniper story is conjured by the author and is a work of fiction, there is a flower farm called, 'The Blooming Barn' in the Comox Valley on Vancouver Island, Canada. Any similarities to actual persons, living or dead, events or locations is coincidental.
All illustrations are the original artwork of Fiona Van Housen.

Audio recorded and edited by Paul Keim at Dove Creek Recording
Editing, layout, and pre-press by Kera McHugh, time4somethingelse.com
Photo of Fiona Van Housen ©Terry Farrell
Photo of Mary Murphy ©Paul Keim
Bumble Bee and Me: lyrics ©Mary Murphy, melody ©Paul Keim
Lullaby: lyrics and melody ©Mary Murphy
Boogie Beat: lyrics ©Mary Murphy, melody ©Paul Keim

To request permission, contact:
mary@marymurphy.ca

ISBN: 978-1-7387936-1-7

Sweet Peas AND Bees

LIFE AT THE FLOWER FARM
Book 1

Illustrated by Fiona Van Housen
Written by Mary Murphy

See page 24 and beyond for extras and a QR code to access bonus audio, directions to The Blooming Barn and more...

When Granny June asked her granddaughter what she would like for her sixth birthday, Juniper replied, "I want to bring summer smiles to people.

May I have flowers to give to some of my friends?"

"What a thoughtful child you are," replied Granny June.

"Do you know what, my little Sweet Pea? I know a place not far from here where you can pick your own flowers. We can go there today, if you like."

4

Juniper leapt from her chair with a squeal, hugged her Granny June tightly, and asked, "Can I bring Roo?"

Granny June smiled. "She's more than welcome to come along, but do you think a full-sized dragon will fit in my little car? Isn't she ten-foot tall with a very long tail?"

Juniper thought about her dragon a moment, clapped her hands and spun around in a circle, proud to have come up with a solution.

"She can scrunch up tight in the back. Her head and tail will have to go out the back windows though."

5

When Juniper and Granny June arrived at their destination, they saw a woman dressed in coveralls outside a small building, arranging bundles of flowers into bouquets.

The sign above the door read, "The Blooming Barn."

The woman, whose hair was bright green and pink, smiled warmly and welcomed them to the flower farm.

The flower lady then bent down to Juniper and pointed to a sea of colour.

"Go right through that gate and you'll be in the field of flowers. Your grandmother and I will follow shortly with a bucket and clippers."

As Juniper closed the gate behind her, she was met with a faint sound of busy bees flitting around to collect their pollen and nectar. A fuzzy, yellow and black bumble bee landed on her shoulder.

"Welcome to the garden," said the bumble bee. "May I join you?"

"Yes, please," answered Juniper, laughing as the lovely, soft hairs of the bumble bee tickled her neck.

"Are you a honey bee?" she asked.

"Great question," buzzed the bumble in reply.

"No, I'm a bumble bee. We look quite different from honey bees—and honey bees live in hives or sometimes in bee boxes. We bumble bees live underground in nests, or holes in logs, or even in burrows that mice or rats used to live in."

Juniper's eyes opened wide with surprise. "Oh, I see," she said, walking toward a nearby row of very tall flowers.

"Oh my!" chirped Juniper. "Do you know what they are? They're so bright and tall."

The bee flew and landed gently upon the petals. "I know all the flowers here. These are called cosmos.

Bumble bees love this flower as it gives us so much nectar. Nectar is what we call our food."

Bumble flew to the next row. These flowers, too, were very tall. "Do you like these?" she asked. "They are sunflowers and everyone seems to love them. Not only are they very pretty, but people can eat the seeds."

10

"Ooh sunflower seeds! They're delicious." said Juniper, excitedly.

Again the bee buzzed happily. "I bet your granny uses sunflower oil when she is cooking. That oil comes from this plant."

11

Juniper looked up to a lone rain cloud above their heads.

Suddenly, the cloud released its drops, and the bumble bee swiftly flew across the path, to the zinnia flowers.

She nestled deep within the petals, tucking her little body around the centre.

The cloudburst did not last long, and Juniper walked to the zinnias calling, "You can come out now!"

The bumble bee shook the moisture off herself and flew out and away toward another row of flowers that were all shades of purple, white, blue, and pink.

"I love these ones," whispered Juniper, as though speaking too loudly might cause the delicate flowers to droop.

"These are sweet peas," buzzed the bee. "They smell delightful, and we bees love them."

Juniper repeated the name, "Sweet peas. My granny calls me Sweet Pea sometimes. She brought me here today."

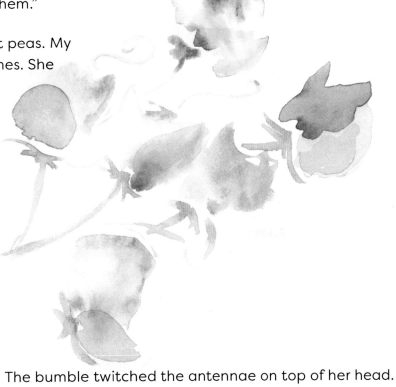

The bumble twitched the antennae on top of her head.

"That's a lovely thing to be called. In flower language, sweet peas are known as flowers of joy and good will, so I'm not surprised she calls you by this name."

"Really? I love my Granny so much, so I will get her some of these."

"Who else do you want to bring flowers to?" asked the bee.

15

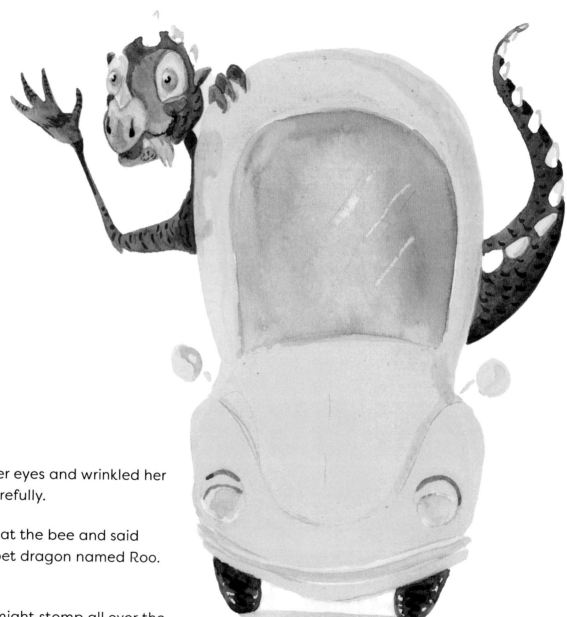

Juniper closed her eyes and wrinkled her nose, thinking carefully.

Then, she looked at the bee and said softly, "I have a pet dragon named Roo. She's in the car.

I was afraid she might stomp all over the flowers by mistake, so I left her there. But, I think she would love some flowers."

16

The bumble buzzed.

"Follow me!" she called, flying so fast that Juniper had to skip to catch up.

"Guess what these are?" asked the bumble. The bee was so excited to have found the perfect flowers for Roo that she did not even wait for Juniper to make a guess.

"SnapDRAGONS!

They come in many colours. If you gently, so gently, squeeze the base of a flower head, it looks like a dragon opening its mouth!"

The bright-haired flower lady, carrying a bouquet filled with dahlias, marigolds, and greenery, tapped Juniper on the shoulder.

"Ahh, I see you have made friends with one of the bumbles. You know, they recognize people they have seen before, especially those who treat them kindly.

I know she'd be very pleased if you returned to my flower field for another visit."

Granny June approached with a black bucket and clippers.

"Oh, we'll be back here every Saturday this summer, won't we, Sweet Pea? Juniper is one busy bee herself, and now that she has a bumble friend, well..."

Juniper, Granny June, and the flower lady walked the garden paths together, clipping flowers and stopping by numerous varieties, including billy buttons, bachelor buttons, statice, and yarrow.

20

"Who might you buy flowers for next Saturday, Juniper?" asked Granny June.

Juniper skipped toward the exit gate, bumble flying alongside her as she called out the names of those she wished to bring flowery joy to:

"Let me think...there's Cameron...and Xavier, Cara and Hans...Zoe...Zepher... Sterling and Malachy... Bridget...I'm coming Roo!...Adil and Isaak...Roma..."

22

Bumble watched as Juniper made her way to Granny's car, and buzzed as loud as she could.

"See you soon, new friend. Thanks for coming! And now... I'm hungry."

And she buzzed off, making her way back to a long row of star flowers.

A few fun flower and bee facts

Bumble bees

There are around 250 species across the world. Bumble bees are approximately 13–15mm long and only make tiny quantities of honey. Their main job is to pollinate. They are highly intelligent and actually know what flowers they have already visited. They will not die if they use their stinger.

Ornamental sweet peas

look and smell really yummy, but don't eat them! They are not good for people or pets! The pea pods look very much like snap peas, (which are good for humans and animals).

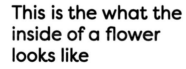

Honey bees

Honey bees can also be found throughout the world. Like their bumble cousins, they are approximately 13–15mm long. When a hive becomes overcrowded, the queen lays eggs in queen cells. When the new queens are almost ready to emerge, the old queen leaves the hive with thousands of worker bees so they can find a new home. They will die if they use their stinger.

This is the what the inside of a flower looks like

Sweat bees

Sweat bees are found worldwide, too. They are about 5–6mm long and do not produce honey, but do pollinate. If you are ever out in the garden and discover you have a tiny bee sitting on your arm, it may well be a sweat bee, as they likely think your sweat is delicious due to the salt content of your skin.

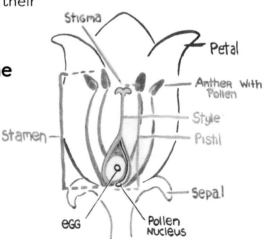

Stigma
Petal
Anther With Pollen
Style
Stamen
Pistil
Sepal
egg
Pollen Nucleus

Busy Bee and me

She flits around the garden - black and yellow
From mornings early hours - until shadow
I dance upon the grasses - listening gleefully
To buzzing bumble rumbles - on the breezes

Busy bumble
Busy friends
Busy bumble
I will hum along with thee

Here is a summer shower - one small rain cloud
She hides in a flower - tucked up inside
I'll wait for a few minutes - stand along side
Then call her back to me when - drops subside

I spread my arms and fingers - as I follow
Pretend that I am flying wherever she goes
My buzzing friend has landed on a star flower
I like that stars can be seen at any hour

This summer day is ending and I must go
Deliver friendship colours to those that I know
I will return again to walk among the flowers
And with my bumble friend we'll wile
   away the hours

Lullaby

Loo la loo la loo la loo la lie
Hushabye lullabye
Loo la loo la loo la loo la lay
Hushabye drowsy babe

Don't ye mind the wind on high
Nor branches groaning deep
Be at peace my little one
As twilight shadow sweep

We shall flit among the lambs
Come April's brightening spring
Cheered by river swans
When summer days do fade

Dandelions have closed their eyes
Droning bees do sleep
Slip inside a mother's song
'til slumber does bequeath

Boogie Beat

Juniper's a girl who loves to dance -
wiggles every time that she gets a chance
doesn't matter if it's day or night -
she'll boogie at sunrise or by firelight

Chubby bee returns to the nest -
she was gone on a blossom quest
"Follow me my sisters, I have found a place -
where petals shimmer and sway with grace."

We are all living on this earth
And each day is brand new birth
Yes we're all living on this earth
Each and every being full of worth

Buzzing bumble holds a steady beat -
tapping out a rhythm on shuffling feet
Wings are flapping at surprising speed -
movin' all the pollen to create a seed

Juniper is walking in-between two rows -
Six foot flowers all yellow and gold
Wavin' to her granny and the lady who -
planted all the joy that has grown so true

Juniper and bumble have the summer free -
to move together in a dancing spree
Jump to the left swing to the right -
filling their time with pure delight

Colours of the rainbow in every shade -
Juniper and bumble in a plant parade
There's not much finer than a loving friend -
who'll move along with you until days end

About the Illustrator, Fiona Van Housen

Fiona Van Housen owns an innate sense of artistry. She has studied under tutelage in Wicklow, Ireland, and attended arts programs in Canada. Whistler Book Awards calls Fiona's work "...entirely enticing...with colours blending beautifully." This is the fourth book Fiona has illustrated; the previous three are for a fairy book series, *Away with the Fairies.* Fiona and her partner, Cameron, own and operate a flower farm, The Blooming Barn (the first and only U-Pick flower farm in the area), in the Comox Valley on Vancouver Island, Canada. They live with their dog Roo, their cat Kitty, and numerous chickens. *Sweet Peas and Bees* is the first of the *Life at the Flower Farm* children's book series. thebloomingbarn.com

Follow @thebloomingbarncv

About the Author, Mary Murphy

Follow @marymurphycreates

This is Ms Murphy's sixth book release. Others include the Fiction/Fantasy novel *The Emerald Diaries – Secrets of an Irish Clan*; *Speaking Of*, a book of eclectic fiction stories; and a children's trilogy, *Away with the Fairies* (with audio). Whistler Book Awards says of Mary's writing, "There is a quality of 'enchantment' that Mary brings through the use of language... writes in an imaginative, lyrical style that is both poetic and evocative." Mary has released thirteen musical CDs. Originally from Wexford Town, Ireland, she now lives and creates on Vancouver Island, Canada, with her husband Paul and is the mother of two grown children. Mary and Paul share their home with their dog Norah and cat Turtle. marymurphy.ca

Who would YOU buy flowers for?

"Sweet Peas and Bees
is utterly charming...
presented beautifully with
illustrations which delight
and draw you in... this book
and audio would make a
sweet and delightful gift."

~ Ruth Buklin, Teacher
Peace Valley Waldorf School

Scan the QR code for:

- One audio book of author reading Sweet Peas and Bees (with character voices)
- Three Songs performed by author
- Song Lyrics
- Videos
- Honey Recipes
- More colouring pages
- Directions to The Blooming Barn, in the Comox Valley, on Vancouver Island, Canada

Sweet Peas

Bumble bee

Zinnia

Manufactured by Amazon.ca
Bolton, ON

34094513R00019